MM at the Movies

Written by Jill Eggleton
Illustrated by Jennifer Cooper

Pop and Harry were going
to the movies.
MM Mouse sat by her cage,
and her whiskers went

wobble, wobble.

"No, MM!" said Harry.
"You can't come."

But MM Mouse was **not**
staying home.
She saw Harry's coat
on the chair,
so she sneaked
into the pocket.

Pop and Harry sat in the movies
with a **big** bag of popcorn.
MM Mouse
sneaked
out of Harry's pocket
and sat under the seat.
It was dark and warm,
and there was popcorn
all over the floor.
MM Mouse loved popcorn.

MM Mouse went

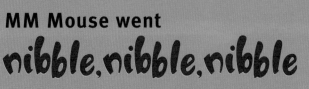

nibble, nibble, nibble

on the popcorn until she couldn't
eat any more.
Then she looked around.

She could see feet – lots of feet.
She loved running over feet.
So off she went – over this foot
and that foot.
Up this leg and that leg.

People screamed . . .

"There's a mouse in here!"

8

The movie stopped and the lights came on. A woman came in with a big flashlight. People were standing on their seats, waving and shouting.

"I will have to get
the mouse catchers then,"
said the woman.
"But they won't come until tomorrow."

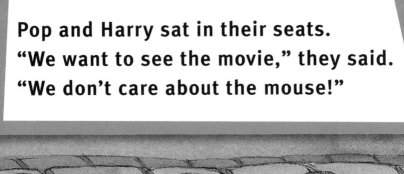

Pop and Harry sat in their seats.
"We want to see the movie," they said.
"We don't care about the mouse!"

12

So the woman put the film on again.
Some people stayed and some people
went home, but everyone
got their money back.
And . . . two free tickets!

At home, after the movie,
Harry took off his coat
and put it on the chair.
"I hope the mouse catchers
don't get that mouse," said Harry.

"We could go and get her," said Pop.
"She would be a friend for MM."

MM's whiskers went

**wobble, wobble,
wobble, wobble,**

and into the air went . . .
a teeny, tiny piece of popcorn.

An Action/Consequence Chart

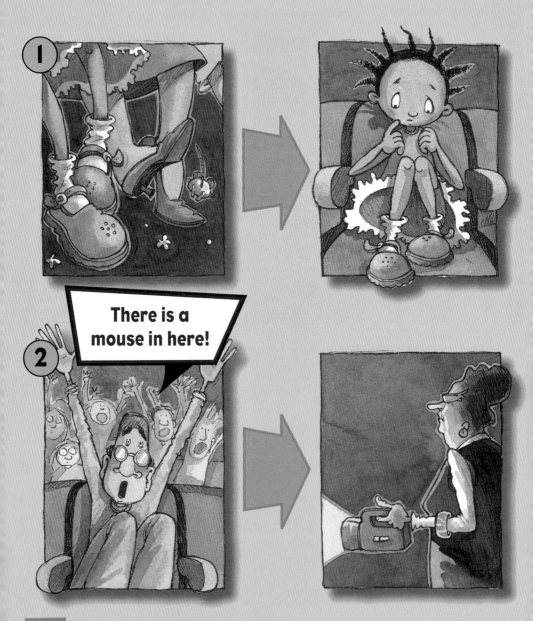

Guide Notes

Title: MM Mouse at the Movies

Stage: Launching Fluency – Orange

Genre: Fiction

Approach: Guided Reading

Processes: Thinking Critically, Exploring Language, Processing Information

Written and Visual Focus: Action/Consequence Chart, Speech Bubbles

Word count: 318

THINKING CRITICALLY
(sample questions)

- What do you think this story could be about? Look at the title and discuss.
- Look at the cover. How do you think MM Mouse got to the movies?
- Look at pages 2 and 3. Why do you think Harry told MM Mouse that she wasn't allowed to come to the movies?
- Look at pages 4 and 5. Why do you think MM Mouse had to sneak out of Harry's coat?
- Look at pages 8 and 9. Why do you think MM Mouse liked running over people's feet?
- Look at pages 10 and 11. How do you think the mouse catchers would catch a mouse?
- Look at pages 12 and 13. Why do you think Pop and Harry said that they didn't care about a mouse being at the movies?
- Look at pages 14 and 15. Why do you think Harry didn't want the mouse catchers to catch the mouse?

EXPLORING LANGUAGE

Terminology
Author and illustrator credits, ISBN number

Vocabulary
Clarify: popcorn, whiskers, movie, tickets
Singular/Plural: whisker/whiskers, ticket/tickets, movie/movies
Homonyms: to/two/too, by/buy, their/there

Print Conventions
Apostrophes – contractions (don't, there's, won't, can't), possessive (Harry's); dashes, ellipses

Phonological Patterns
Focus on short and long vowels **a** (st**a**ying, c**a**ge, b**a**ck)
Discuss endings and root words (runn**ing**, wav**ing**, stopp**ed**)